HIDE AND SEEK

KATIE MAY GREEN

For Matt and Leo,
with my love.

A new day begins.

WALKER BOOKS
AND SUBSIDIARIES
LONDON • BOSTON • SYDNEY • AUCKLAND

First published 2019
by Walker Books Ltd
87 Vauxhall Walk
London SE11 5HJ

This edition published 2020

2 4 6 8 10 9 7 5 3 1

© 2019 Katie May Green

The right of Katie May Green to be identified as
author/illustrator of this work has been asserted by her in
accordance with the Copyright, Designs and Patents Act 1988

This book has been typeset in Poliphilus MT • Printed in China

British Library Cataloguing in Publication Data:
a catalogue record for this book is available from the British Library

ISBN 978-1-4063-9301-9 • www.walker.co.uk

Right at the top
of Shiverhawk Hall
live children in pictures
on the wall.

Peeking out, woken gently
by a midsummer moon,
they spot something strange
about their room:

the *twins* have vanished
from their picture frame!
Where could they be?
It's time for a game...

"HIDE AND SEEK!" cries Percy.

Lily says, "Whoopeee!"

"Let's find the twins!"

say the Plumseys, all three.

Billy starts the countdown

while the others look for clues.

"10-9-8-7-6-5-4-3-2-1...

"WE'RE COMING

TO FIND YOU!"

The friends run riot through the warm night air,

hunting white ribbons and long black hair.

"I've found the twins! Look up here!" laughs Lily,

and Percy says, "No, they're just statues, silly!"

Then the SPLASHING begins ... and no one can see

two clever girls hiding, quiet as can be.

Squeezing out through the wall they find their way
and there, in the wild of the woods, they play.

Spying birds up above, spotting bugs down below,

but no sign of the twins, so onwards they go …

until they arrive at the best place of all! "Let's play here forever!" the children call.

Then, all of a sudden … there's a sneeze from the bushes! Some giggling, too!

What could it be? Could it be – YOU KNOW WHO?!

Percy gasps … hops closer … and—

"FOUND

The Shiverhawk children
have found their two friends.
"My turn to hide now!" cheers Percy.
"Let's play it again!"

But just at that moment
the sky starts to tremble,
to rumble,
to CRASH!

And –
plip
plop
   plip *plop*
plip *plop* *plip* *plop* *plip* *plop* *plip* *plop*...

A thunder bolt, a lightning flash!
"Oh no! We're so far from home!
It's time to get back!"

So they slip and squelch back through their forest of fun,

waving, *Bye-bye, birds! Bye-bye, bugs!* and homeward they run...

With muddy wet ribbons and soggy black hair,

the two lead their friends through the damp dawn air.

The twins are first in,
scrambling up to their room,
then it's Lily, then Billy,
then the Plumseys, and soon

they call down to Percy,
"Be quick! Climb in!"

And the rain starts to soften —
plip plop
        plip
            plop
                plip—
The sun's on its way …
a new day will begin.

And so into their frames
the children sneak,
'til the next time they play …

Hide and Seek.